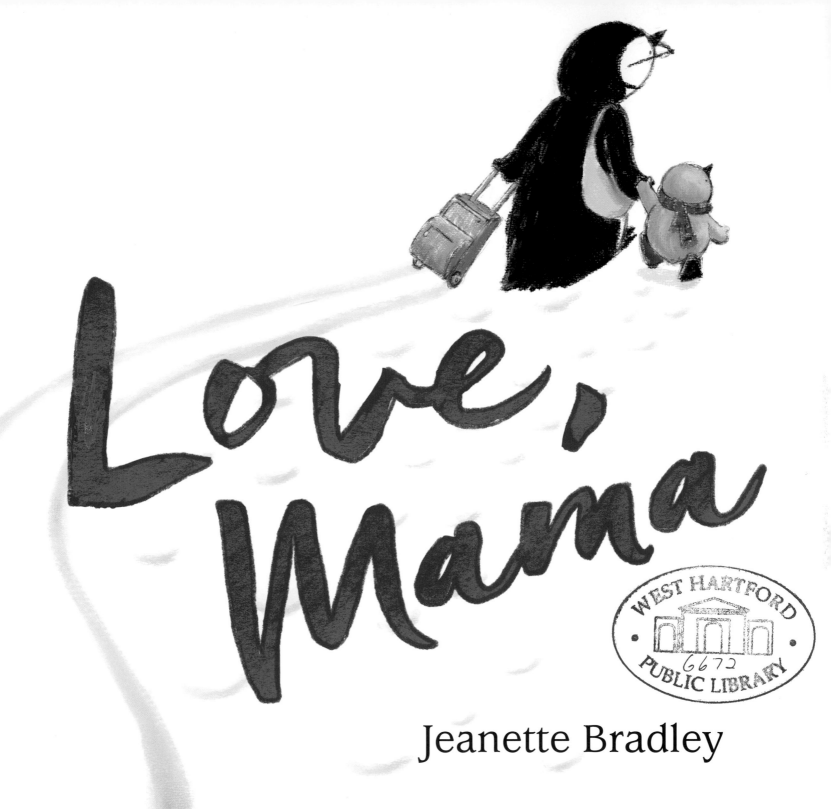

Love, Mama

Jeanette Bradley

ROARING BROOK PRESS

New York

For my hatchlings, with love

Copyright © 2018 by Jeanette Bradley
Published by Roaring Brook Press
Roaring Brook Press is a division of Holtzbrinck Publishing Holdings Limited Partnership
175 Fifth Avenue, New York, NY 10010
mackids.com

Library of Congress Control Number: 2017944504

ISBN 978-1-62672-949-0

Our books may be purchased in bulk for promotional, educational, or business use. Please
contact your local bookseller or the Macmillan Corporate and Premium Sales Department at
(800) 221-7945 ext. 5442 or by e-mail at MacmillanSpecialMarkets@macmillan.com.

First edition, 2018
Book design by Kristie Radwilowicz
Printed in China by RR Donnelley Asia Printing Solutions Ltd.,
Dongguan City, Guangdong Province

10 9 8 7 6 5 4 3 2 1

JJ
BRADLEY
JEANETTE

When they reached the ocean,
Kipling waved goodbye to Mama.
She called, "I'll be back home soon!"

But Mama didn't come home for dinner.

Or at bedtime.

In the morning, Kipling
looked everywhere for Mama.

But Pillow Mama
wouldn't read,

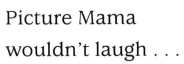

Picture Mama
wouldn't laugh . . .

. . . and Snow Mama was too cold to cuddle.

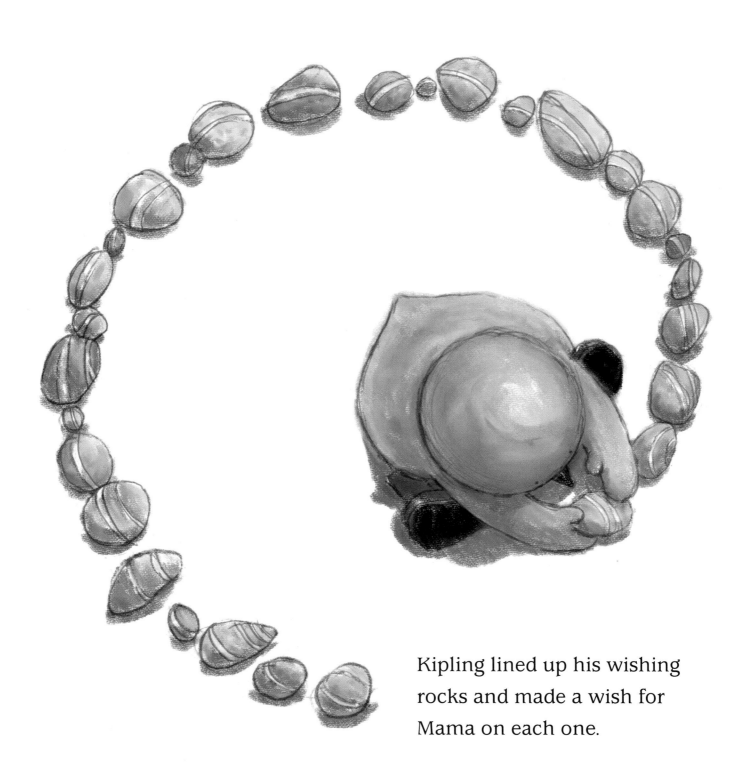

Kipling lined up his wishing
rocks and made a wish for
Mama on each one.

He waited and waited, but not even
one Wish Mama came home.

Then the doorbell rang.
It wasn't Mama.
It was just a sad, soggy box.

Kipling shook the box.
It rustled and thunked
and smelled like the sea.

He peeked inside.

It was from Mama! She had sent him a box of his favorite things, and a paper heart that read:

My love for you stretches across the wide ocean,

through day

and night,

from earth
to sky
and back again,

from my heart to yours.
Love, Mama

Kipling hugged the
heart, just like Mama
in the picture.

Then Kipling found his own box
and made his own heart for Mama.

His wish for Mama
would stretch from
earth to sky,

through day and night,

across the wide ocean . . .

. . . and back again.

Mama!
She was home at last.

Mama was home for dinner,
and bedtime . . .

. . . and all the
hugs in between.